EOIN
McLAUGHLIN

ROSS
COLLINS

INSPECTOR
PENGUIN
INVESTIGATES

ORCHARD

BEHOLD –
THE DIAMONDO DEL MONDO.

The largest and most glittery diamond in the world.
WATCH IT GLITTER! SEE IT SPARKLE!

The diamond belongs to **BARON VON BUFFETWORTH.**

"Get away. Do you even have permission to be in here?"

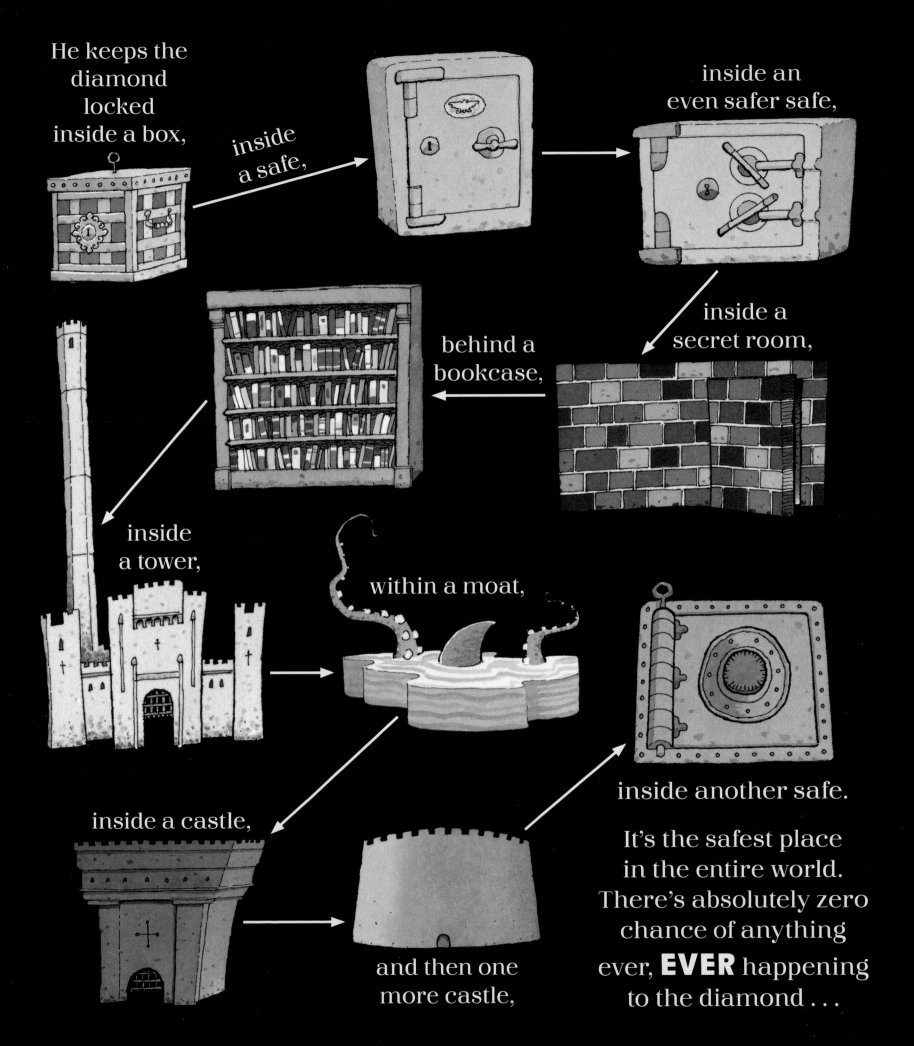

He keeps the diamond locked inside a box,

inside a safe,

inside an even safer safe,

inside a secret room,

behind a bookcase,

inside a tower,

within a moat,

inside a castle,

and then one more castle,

inside another safe.

It's the safest place in the entire world. There's absolutely zero chance of anything ever, **EVER** happening to the diamond . . .

SOUND THE ALARM!
SHUT ALL THE DOORS!
EXTREME PANIC!

THE BARON'S DIAMOND HAS BEEN STOLEN!

It goes without saying, we need **A DETECTIVE.** The most highly trained and super-intelligent detective in the world.

KNOCK KNOCK

That's better.
Right this way please,
Inspector Penguin. Now,
you'll need to find some clues . . .

That's not a clue, that's a fish.

That's also a fish.

That's another fish.

They're more fish.

What's with all the fish?
You're attracting seagulls!

WHAT WE NEED IS A CLUE!

Wait. That **IS** a clue. It's the thief's handprints!
But who could they belong to?

There were only five people here when the
diamond went missing. Let's do a line-up.

Whose hands match the prints, Inspector?

Samna Stern
(the guard)

TOO BIG.

Delia Doorknob
(the maid)

TOO FINGERY.

Francesca de la Huge Mouth
(an opera singer)

TOO . . . NOT THERE

Mr Gumpus
(the baron's butler)

IT'S A MATCH!
Well spotted, Inspector!
You've caught him red-pawed!

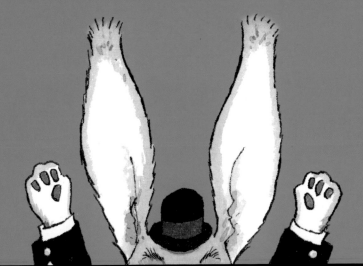

Mr Gumpus . . . you're under arrest.

Wait. He's escaping.

Hmmm . . .

you're not really . . .

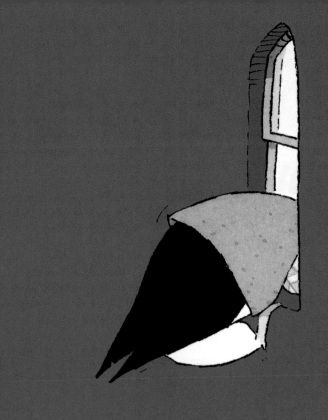

built for speed . . .   are you?

WOW.

That's more like it!
Nice slide, you slippery sleuth.

Diddlesticks. This market is far too crowded.
Can you spot the suspect, Inspector?

Inspector, can you spot him?

INSPECTOR?

Follow him,
Inspector Penguin.

**HE'S IN
THAT CAB!**

ON THAT BICYCLE!

THAT TRAIN!

THAT HOT-AIR BALLOON!

Drat. Mr Gumpus has got
away again. But it looks
like he's left some CLUES . . .

Hmmm . . .

OF COURSE! THE DOCKS!

Inspector Penguin, you're a genius!

GOTCHA!
Mr Gumpus, you're under arrest!
Now hand over the diamond!

I don't know
what you're talking
about. I'm just
going on holiday.

FISH

Hmm. We've searched him and there's no diamond. He's clean.

"I had a bath last night."

You've got the wrong suspect, Inspector Penguin. You're clearly not the brilliant detective we thought you were.

WAIT –

Inspector Penguin?

FISH

Oh my halibut! The diamond! You did it, Inspector Penguin. You're the best detective in the **WHOLE WIDE WORLD!**

"Elementary, my dear tuna."

And, look, here's the baron. He would like to present
you with a **MEDAL OF HONOUR.**

For he's a jolly good penguin,
For he's a jolly good penguin,

For he's a jolly good—

HOLD ON.

Where's he going?

Inspector Penguin?

W O DID IT?

1. Did you see Delia Doorknob take the diamond from the safe . . .

2. . . . and hide it under the carpet?

3. Then Francesca de la Huge Mouth hid it inside her cheek . . .

4. . . . and snuck it out of the castle . . .

5. . . . before Samna Stern drove it down to the docks . . .

6. . . . where Mr Gumpus was going to take it on board the ship and sell it to pay for unlimited rides for all of them on the 100 greatest waterslides in the world!

ORCHARD BOOKS

First published in Great Britain in 2021 by The Watts Publishing Group
10 9 8 7 6 5 4 3 2 1

Text © Eoin McLaughlin 2021 / Illustrations © Ross Collins 2021

The moral rights of the author and illustrator have been asserted.
All rights reserved.

A CIP catalogue record for this book is available from the British Library.

HB ISBN 978 1 40835 430 8 / PB ISBN 978 1 40835 431 5

Printed and bound in China

Orchard Books. An imprint of Hachette Children's Group
Part of The Watts Publishing Group Limited

Carmelite House, 50 Victoria Embankment, London EC4Y 0DZ
An Hachette UK Company

www.hachette.co.uk / www.hachettechildrens.co.uk

FSC
www.fsc.org

MIX
Paper from
responsible sources
FSC® C104740